Who Will Haunt My House on Halloween?

Jerry Pallotta

SCHOLASTIC INC.
Cartwheel BOOKS®

New York   Toronto   London   Auckland
Sydney   Mexico City   New Delhi   Hong Kong

David Biedrzycki

For trick-or-treaters — Sheila, Neil, Eric, and Jill!
-J.P.

To Wouter Laleman — he's such a good librarian, it's scary!
-D.B.

ISBN 978-0-545-31192-2

Text copyright © 2007 by Jerry Pallotta.
Illustrations copyright © 2007 by David Biedrzycki.
All rights reserved. Published by Scholastic Inc.
SCHOLASTIC, CARTWHEEL BOOKS, and associated logos are trademarks and/or registered trademarks of Scholastic Inc.

12 11 10 9 8 7 6 5 4 3 2 1   10 11 12 13 14 15/0

Printed in the U.S.A.   08
First Scholastic paperback printing, October 2010

It's Halloween!

I'm scared!

I wonder who will haunt my house tonight?

Werewolves might trick-or-treat.

They would howl at the moon. *Aaah! Oooooooooh!*

Maybe scary ghosts will show up.

They can take the candy. I'll stay away from them.

Oh, no! Zombies!

Please stop! I'm afraid of real live dead people.

Uh-oh! Spooky bats!

Run! Run! RUN! There are zillions of them.

Now I'm really scared! This isn't funny.

I'm not touching their bony fingers.

Wow! Jack-o'-lanterns are everywhere!

They've left me a spooky message!

Owls might visit!

Hoot! That's right! *Hoot!* They love to fly at night!

Dinosaurs? What are you doing here?

You're extinct!

Help! Scarecrows aren't supposed to walk!

Back off! No birds allowed in this house!

"Did anyone trick-or-treat yet?" asks my mom.

"No, it's been very quiet."

Ding dong! Someone's at the door!

Let's all go trick-or-treating! What fun!

We are on our way to haunt your house! Happy Halloween!